for my ACE MUM! with lots of love

Read the whole series:

This book
belongs to...

DOT

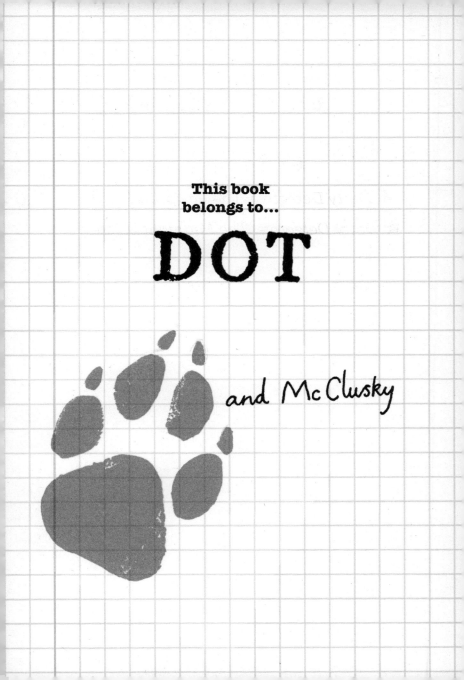

and McClusky

Sunday

This is me!

My real name is Dorothy Constance Mae Louise, but that's a bit of a mouthful so I just like to be called Dot.

I might SEEM as if I have an ordinary sort of life. I live with my mum, the twins (my brother and sister Alf and Maisy) and my dog, McClusky...

and I go to Oakfield School.

BUT **THAT'S** NOT ALL... Me and
McClusky and my best pal, Beans,
have our very own super-secret,
super-sleuthing detective agency:
the JOIN THE DOTS DETECTIVES!

However murky the mystery or
fiendishly puzzling the problem,
we can **ALWAYS** piece together the
clues and solve the case. It's like
a really complicated join the dots
puzzle: only at the *end* can you see
the whole picture.

TOP
SECRET
★

Here is my bedroom – check out the amazing chandelier Mum gave me!

This isn't just my bedroom, though, **OH NO**. *It's also the Join the Dots Detectives HQ, where I do all my best deductivising, head scratching and end-of-pencil chewing when I am on a case and studying the clues.*

Join the Dots Detectives HQ

I keep all my treasures here too. LOTS of boxes, packed full to bursting with all my special things.

Mum says it drives her CRAZY that we all have TOO MUCH STUFF in our family.

Although one look at her collection of unusual teapots

and it is clear that she has A LOT of stuff too.

The twins have their own weird collections...

and, when me and Mum move the furniture to do the hoovering, we discover that McClusky has been hoarding HIS "treasures" too, behind the sofa.

"So that's where my knitting wool has got to!" says Mum.

McClusky's embarrassed face!

Monday

Coconut Crunchies for breakfast!

YESSSSSS!!!

It's my **BEST** and **FAVOURITE** cereal. I do the maze on the back of the packet.

Mum says, "A new week!" and turns over a page on our wall calendar. It says, *Life is a gift – enjoy every moment!*

But the twins are enjoying every moment of putting on all their clothes **COMPLETELY INSIDE OUT** a bit too much, so now we are in a HUGE rush to get to school on time.

Lining up in the playground to go into our classrooms, there is only one thing everybody is talking about...

On Wednesday we are going on a school trip! **THREE WHOLE DAYS** at ADVENTURE CAMP!!!

"I haven't been away to any kind of camp before," says Amy nervously. "I wonder what it will be like?"

"I've been on **LOADS** of camps," Laura says, "and I've gone night-kayaking in the Amazon **AND** slept under the stars in the Arctic!"

Laura ALWAYS gets on our nerves.

I ignore Laura and say to Amy, "Me neither, but I am sure it's going to be *brilliant!*"

"It's not as far as the Amazon, but it's definitely a long way away," says Beans. *"TWO HOURS* in the school coach!"

After registration our teacher Mr Dickens is telling us more about the trip.

Mr D tells us that we will be put into groups for sleeping, with separate cabins for girls and for boys.

PLEASE, PLEASE, PLEASE *no snorers in*

my cabin, I am saying to myself!

Z Z Z Z Z Z Z Z Z Z Z Z

We will also be put into different teams for the activities. There will be **points** given for each activity, and also for being helpful and tidy, and the team with the most points wins...

THE ACE ADVENTURERS' PRIZE!!!

ACE!

Laura says she has won first prize for snowboarding and for horse riding AND for abseiling and she will **DEFINITELY** win the **ACE ADVENTURERS' PRIZE** too.

Mr D is looking at the list of activities, making WOW faces and gasps of astonishment.

"The activities are **TOP SECRET** until we get there!" says Mr D, creating a big show of turning the piece of paper face down on his desk so we cannot see. "But here's a little clue..."

Mr D does his special suspense
dance. He loves teasing us!

"We will have close encounters with
NATURE ON THE WILD SIDE,"
he says, "and explore our spirit of
adventure!"

This sounds amazing! Everybody is
cheering.

Frankie Logan who sits at my table
is over-keen to show us his wild side
and ends up falling off his chair.

"We will have

NIGHT-TIME
ESCAPADES!"

Mr D goes on.

Everybody is going crazy with excitement.

"And now," he says, holding up some jam jars full of leaves – I can just make out something moving inside – "to get us in the mood for the **Adventure Camp Nature Trail...**

23

"Let's show some **love** for BUGS AND SLUGS!"

By now some people are **literally** screaming. What will it be like when we actually *get there???*

Breaktime and I'm heading out to the playground, but I forgot my tangerine so I go back to the classroom.

But when I walk in through the door...

I see Laura in the empty classroom. She has turned over the activities list on Mr D's desk and she's **reading** it.

I get a **FUNNY FEELING**, beginning in my toes. Before she can see me I quietly back out of the room and *rush* to find Beans.

"Laura was sneaking a look at the list," I say to Beans. "It looked

VERY FISHY to me..."

"Sounds **DODGY** to me too," agrees Beans. "Why does she want to know what the activities are, ahead of everybody else?"

We don't know what to make of it. But one thing's for sure... when Laura is hatching one of her DEVIOUS PLANS, it always spells trouble for everybody else.

In the lunch hall, sitting with Amy and

Beans, Amy is still feeling **anxious** about the trip, so Beans cheers her up by sharing his pineapple chunks with her.

At the next table Laura is writing in her sparkly pink secret notebook and looking over at us.

The funny feeling has reached my stomach. I don't like the look of this ONE BIT.

In Geography we are doing map-making. Beans is **genius** at maps. We make a key of *official* symbols:

FOOTPATH   ---------

WALKS

RAILWAY AND STATION

VIEWPOINT

LIGHTHOUSE

CASTLE

WOODS

POND

GRASSLANDS

CAMPSITE

And we make up some of our own too...

LAURA

BEAR

EMERGENCY SNACKS

MARSHMALLOWS

MYSTERY ???

SPACESHIP

At going-home time Mr D gives us all a reminder **KIT LIST** to take home.

I still need to get a few **extremely important** things like toothpaste and a new raspberry-scented gel pen... so I ask Mum if we can walk home via the high street.

As we go past the pet-grooming parlour Paws Awhile, I see a poster in the window:

This particularly catches my eye. I look at the different categories... Which could McClusky win?

He IS the most handsome dog in the whole world, surely! Hmmmm, but he does look as though he's been pulled through a hedge backwards... I would LOVE to buy him a new brush – and there are bow ties for dogs too! SO many to choose from! But I don't have enough pocket money.

Maybe!

OH NO. I think McClusky would eat it immediately!

But whatever his chances I will **DEFINITELY** enter McClusky into the Larks in the Park Dog Show. We will begin a *strict training programme* tonight. Mum will have to take over while I'm away on **Adventure Camp**, though.

At home I decorate the kit list with my BEST stickers and put it up on the fridge with a dotty magnet.

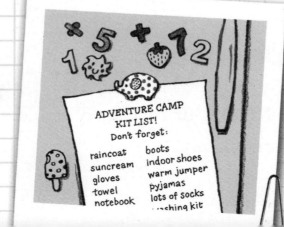

ADVENTURE CAMP
KIT LIST!
Don't forget:

raincoat   boots
suncream   indoor shoes
gloves   warm jumper
towel   pyjamas
notebook   lots of socks
                     ...shing kit

We have spaghetti for tea. The twins are seeing who can make the most noise **slurping** up each strand.

"You have the table manners of a couple of piglets!" says Mum.

After tea I do Waggiest Tail practice with McClusky. For just *HALF* a Doggylicious biscuit let me tell you it's actually **IMPOSSIBLE** to count the wags!

I'm starting to pack my suitcase.
Every time I tick one thing off the kit
list, I think of two new things to add.

AT LEAST 4 or 5 puzzle books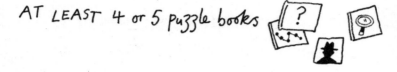

The BEST things from my
stationery collection

VITAL to have hair slides
in every colour

"Vital? REALLY?" says Mum,
popping her head round the door.

Then she says, "Here – I've bought you a new sponge bag for your trip!" It has cats wearing glasses on it, writing letters and numbers.

7
8
2
3   15
5
9
6   11
12
23

Mum says it's really a pencil case, but they are the same thing and no one will notice.

The twins wish they were going on **Adventure Camp**. They make a den out of sheets from the washing basket...

and do

EXTREME

SPORTS on the sofa,

even though they are not allowed
since they broke the springs
practising the Olympic long jump.

At bedtime, I'm thinking about Laura acting strangely at school. Is she planning something SNEAKY???

boasting about
winning first prize

sneaking a look at the
top secret activities list

writing in her secret notebook

All very odd...

Trying new hairstyles helps me to relax. Doing my hair with one bobble...

and with three bobbles... but two is

BEST.

Tuesday

I need to talk to Beans again about Laura, but there is **NO TIME** because straight away after registration it is PE in the playground.

We are practising our

WILD-SIDE running.

We pretend we are running through the forest, dodging dangerous animals, deep rivers and cliff edges.

Mr D shouts out commands, like "JUMP OVER LOGS!" and

"DUCK UNDER BRANCHES!"

It is seriously full of perils. Joe falls into a "pit of snakes" and Beth is "carried off by a bear".

In quiet reading, we are finding it hard to concentrate. Just one day to go!!!

Beans whispers to me, "WHAT

SWEETS ARE YOU BRINGING ON THE COACH? I AM BRINGING CHOCO CHOOS," and I whisper back, "SUPER-SOUR APPLE SHERBETS!"

We don't notice Mr D is standing behind us. But instead of telling us off he whispers loudly, "AND I WILL

BE BRINGING TREACLE TOFFEE
BON-BONS."

In PSHE Mr D talks to us about
being away from home. He tells us
that feeling worried or a bit homesick
is totally *fine* and nothing to be
embarrassed about.

Laura says she has been away from
home for **WEEKS AND WEEKS**
and doesn't get homesick *at all*.

Amy is very quiet.

I'm definitely going to miss Mum.

43

And I realise I haven't been away from McClusky for **three whole days**

EVER!

For tea I ask Mum extra-nicely if we can have sausages so I can do some sausage-on-a-plate practice with McClusky.

He actually manages to catapult the sausage into the air, drop the plate, catch the sausage and eat it, all in about ONE SECOND.

Impressive, but not *quite* what the judges are looking for.

After tea I watch this week's episode of **FRED FANTASTIC – ACE DETECTIVE.**

Me and Beans both think it is the best TV programme **EVER**.

Fred is a detective who solves fiendishly tricky crimes by finding clues and piecing them together, just like the **JOIN THE DOTS DETECTIVES** do.

We *ALWAYS* follow **FRED FANTASTIC'S** five golden rules for solving a case:

⭐ 1 **STAY FROSTY.**
This means STAY ALERT.
Fred Fantastic says this a lot.

2 **FOLLOW THAT HUNCH!**
Always listen to your
instincts because they could
lead to something.

3 **USE YOUR NOODLE.**
Use your brain – think!

4 **LOOK FOR A LIGHT-BULB
MOMENT.**
A brilliant idea to help you
suss things out.

5 **GET PROOF.**
You always need to have
evidence before coming to any
crafty conclusions.

47

In this episode a dastardly villain switches the road signs so that Fred and his cool sidekick, Flo, drive straight off the jetty and into the sea!

DOT'S ROOM

Now I MUST finish my packing!

I have to really SQUEEEEEEEEEZE *everything into the suitcase and sit on it to get the lid shut.*

48

dottiest clothes

wellies

spotty raincoat

cats-in-glasses spongebag

best pyjamas with flamingos on

camera

sunglasses

stationery and puzzle books

"Would you like to borrow my wallaby woolly hat?" asks Mum.

"No more room!" I say. *PHEW* lucky escape!!!

Cannot get to sleep. I am **EXCITED** because I'm looking forward to Adventure Camp SO MUCH. But I am nervous too.

Maybe it's nothing, but I still feel

UNEASY *about Laura.*

And I suddenly realise...

Me and Beans need a really good way to pass secret messages to each other at **Adventure Camp!** *Something small, because we don't have space in our suitcases to take our complete detecting kit.*

I look in my best code book for inspiration, and I have the perfect idea...

A picture code!!

I make a special **picture code**
for us to use:

a	b	c	d	e	f	g
h	i	j	k	l	m	n
o	p	q	r	s	t	u
v	w	x	y	z		

52

I write it twice: once for me and once for Beans. I just try it out to see if it works.

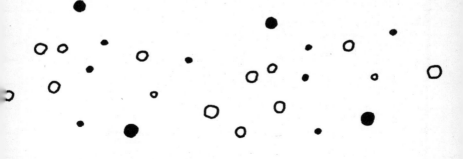

WEDNESDAY

We arrive at school very early in the morning. The coach is already waiting.

While the bags are being loaded on, I super-quickly show the picture code to Beans and give him his copy.

"This way we can send SECRET MESSAGES to each other, just in case..." I whisper.

"BRILLIANT!" whispers Beans.

Mum gives me a **HUGE** hug, then she and the twins and McClusky are smiling and waving and tail-wagging with the other families as we all climb on board.

"Keep up the training practice, McClusky!" I call out from the top step.

And we're OFF!

55

First there are **shrieks**, **whoops** and **cheers**, then three different sing-alongs all at once, and we haven't even got round the corner yet!

Maybe too many sweets have been eaten too quickly BECAUSE...

I don't even want to *think* about what has just happened at the back, but Mr D jumps up and rushes down the aisle with a paper bag. Me and Amy sit together and play a good game of **Fortunately–Unfortunately**.

"Fortunately our private jet lands on a desert island," I say.

"Unfortunately we are immediately surrounded by wolves!" says Amy.

"Fortunately the wolves are very friendly and bring us **CAKE!**" I say.

Amy is feeling a bit **wobbly**.
"Will there be wolves at

Adventure Camp?" she asks.

"I'm SURE there won't be!" I reassure
her.

AT LAST we arrive, and are greeted
by super-friendly young grown-ups
with **Ace Adventure Helper**
written on their T-shirts.

With our outstandingly clever new
map skills we will soon find our way
around!

ADVENTURE CAMP

← high ropes

pond

woods

quiet area

play area

log seating

Snowy → Owl Cabin

Dormouse Cabin →

Golden → Eagle Cabin

games barn

Gazelle Cabin →

canteen

I am in Gazelle Cabin. I'm sharing my cabin with Amy, Kirstie, Alisha and

(OH NO!!!!!)

Laura and her friend Ruby.

Beans is next door, in Golden Eagle Cabin, with Joe, Fiyaz, Marcus, Milo and Frankie.

I **JUST** have time while no one is looking to write a quick **picture code** message to Beans and slip it under the door of his cabin...

There are three sets of bunk beds and three small cupboards next to each bunk. I am sharing bunks with Alisha.

★ I AM SHARING WITH LAURA! WORSE LUCK BUT AT LEAST I CAN KEEP AN EYE ON HER!

61

We have to make our own beds, which includes putting the duvet covers on – NO EASY TASK,

I can tell you...

My duvet is **big** and **lumpy** up one end but empty at the other, and Alisha has completely disappeared inside hers, blundering about like a noisy snowman!

Unpacking, I find in the pocket of my favourite jeans a photo of me and McClusky!

Missing you already!
Mum xxx

Mum must have put it in my suitcase when I wasn't looking! I am **SO PLEASED**. I put it safely under my pillow.

Amy has brought a **cuddly** toy mouse called Mouse. Laura and Ruby are looking over at Mouse and I can see that behind their hands they are laughing.

We walk over to the canteen for lunch, which is a buffet of all kinds of sandwiches, and yoghurts for pudding.

Mr D has changed into a

WILD

orange-and-yellow tracksuit. He looks like a **CRAZY** fruit salad.

He tells us our teams for the activities – I am with Alisha, Beans and Joe.

There is a scoreboard written up with coloured chalk. Everybody is asking, 'Who will win the **ACE ADVENTURERS' PRIZE???'**

The afternoon activity is announced: a high ropes course!

"Points are given for *SPEED*, but also for being good team players and encouraging each other," our Ace Adventure Helpers tell us.

We get into our teams, put on our
helmets and safety harnesses
and away we go!

Up the Jacob's Ladder...

across the rope bridge...

wobble

wobble

and –

WHEEEEEEE!!!!!!

DOWN THE ZIP WIRE!

That was **EXTREMELY** fun! We all collapse on the grass laughing. *CORRECTION* – all except Laura, who is oddly quiet.

At tea our **Ace Adventure Helpers** tell us about our evening activity: campfire stories and marshmallow-toasting!

The Helpers build a brilliant campfire for us. Tiny embers float up and glow all orange-y against the dark night sky.

We sit in a circle round the fire toasting our marshmallows, and each team chooses a person to tell a story.

First Beth tells a really good story about a beluga whale who plays the

bongos.

Then Fiyaz tells a **CRAZY** story about a hundred-metre-wide doughnut from space landing on top of Oakfield School.

Our team has chosen ME! I tell
everyone that mine will be a
SPOOKY story. And so I begin...

"There was once an old falling-down
house with boarded-up windows and
nobody lived there, but in the **dead of
night** sometimes you can hear—"

Then all of a sudden Laura starts **coughing** loudly.

I carry on: "You can hear a strange *wailing* noise and see—"

cough cough

"and see a glimmer of candlelight moving through the cracks—"

* cough cough cough*

I try to carry on with my story, but Laura starts complaining: "The campfire is **too smoky!**" I see her nudging Ruby, who starts coughing too.

"OH NO!" say the Helpers. "Perhaps we need to finish up here and call it a day."

So I never get to finish my story.

"That was really **bad luck**, Dot," says Mr D. I do get some points for trying, but on the scoreboard our team are quite near the bottom now. We are VERY disappointed.

 It must be the middle of the night. I am woken by a noise...

I super-quietly get out of bed and creep to the door. There's a piece of paper on the floor – it's a 𝕞𝕖𝕤𝕤𝕒𝕘𝕖 from Beans!

Laura is **SO SNEAKY!!!!**

I must speak to Beans about this
tomorrow at breakfast.

Thursday

Up and dressed and into the canteen for breakfast. I help myself to bread rolls and jam and pile up a plate with fruit. **Yummy!**

I sit with Beans for a super-hasty **JOIN THE DOTS DETECTIVES** meeting.

"Laura MUST have ruined my spooky campfire story on purpose!" I say. "But why?"

"What if she is trying to stop us winning points so that SHE can win the **ACE ADVENTURES' PRIZE?**" says Beans.

"Yes, I am certain you're right! But before we can be sure, we need proof. This is a case for the Join the Dots Detectives!" I say. "We must **USE OUR PEEPERS** to see what she is planning next."

ON THE CASE

"**STAY FROSTY**, Dot!" says Beans.

"**STAY FROSTY**, Beans!" I say back.

Mr D comes in with a box.
Everyone has a letter from home!

Mine is a card with two elephants
riding a tandem on it, and it says...

Dear Dot,

We hope you are having a **BRILLIANT** time at Adventure Camp!

Don't worry about McClusky's training. I'm sure he will win the Dog Show. AND he will have a surprise to show you when you get home.

See you on Friday – can't wait!

With lots and lots of love, ♡ ♡ ♡

Mum,

🖋 (Alf)   🖋 (Maisy)

and   (McClusky)

XXXX

A SURPRISE?

How mysterious!

But no time to think about that now...

We are going grass

tobogganing!!!

SUCH a **big** climb up the hill – it's practically Mount Everest. SO WINDY at the top, but totally worth it...

I have two goes on my own and one sharing a toboggan with Alisha – we are as squished together as sardines!

Amy is a **bundle of nerves,** but luckily she is in Kirstie's team so they go in a toboggan together too.

HURTLING down the hill *bump **bump bump*** – very fast and VERY FUN!

OOPS! Going too fast!

Lunch is pizza and salad.

DELISH!

Mr D is having a BUSY DAY sorting things out...

Fiyaz's tooth has fallen out and he can't find it, Lily is walking with a mysterious limp and the wind has blown Marcus's hat away.

We can just see it in a nearby field, being trodden on by a cow.

Our afternoon activity is the
**Adventure Camp Nature
Trail**, round the pond and into
the Sensory Garden.

Joe steps nearly up to his knees
in a **boggy puddle**.

At least Amy's happy that there's no
sign of wolves, but we DO see some
frogspawn, a pebble with a hole in it
and an earwig.

Beans calls the earwig Norman
and wonders if he can take it home.
But Norman crawls off and I have a
feeling we will never see him again.

Now we reach the

Sensory Path.

We have bare feet and a blindfold,
so we can experience everything
using our senses of touch and smell.

I explore the feeling of bark
chippings under my feet, the smell
of mud and grass and

something else...

It is Joe's

OLD BOGGY SOCKS,

taken off and **abandoned**. A pretty

powerful

sensory

experience

in itself.

After tea our evening activity is announced:

a moonlight walk!

"When it is completely dark," the Ace Adventure Helpers tell us, "each team will be given a torch. Then we will go out into the night and listen out for **OWLS AND BATS!**"

"But please take extra care when moving around," they say. "It gets REALLY **dark** out there at night!"

Each team has a special pack, laid out on the table, which includes:

a notebook

a pencil

a torch

But when I've cleared away my plate and cup and go to collect our team pack...

our torch has

COMPLETELY

DISAPPEARED!

I see LAURA is lurking nearby.

Other teams' torches are

MISSING too.

I make a

THIS IS URGENT

face at Beans

and he makes a

YES IT IS face back,

but there's no time to talk because we are all madly searching for the missing torches.

But no luck – no sign of them **anywhere**.

The Helpers say we cannot do the moonlight walk if some teams don't have torches.

SO

disappointing.

We all moan and groan, Laura loudest of all.

We all troop into the Games Barn instead.

The Helpers bring trays of lovely **hot chocolate** for us, and their guitars for a

sing-song.

...mmmmm......

Who knew Mr D was **such** a GENIUS on the tambourine?!

At bedtime we are just heading back to our cabins. They look really pretty with fairy lights around the door.

At least the mystery limp is solved...

It turns out Lily and Amber have the same shoes but in **different** sizes, so they thought it would be fun to wear one big one and one little one each.

"You're a **STRANGE** lot," says Mr D, shaking his head and laughing.

We are all getting ready for bed.

Laura and Ruby are whispering in their bunk and rustling packets of crisps. It sounds as though they're having a midnight feast. I wonder where they got their snacks from?

Amy is feeling a bit **wobbly** again. "Are there any bears in these woods?" she asks.

I hear Laura and Ruby stifling **sniggers**.

Me, Kirstie and Alisha all sit on Amy's bunk and chat about other things to distract her. None of us remembered to bring a **midnight**

feast, but Kirstie shares half a bag of pink chocolate penguins left over from the coach journey.

Mr D pops his head round the door to tell us it's time for lights out. He also tells us that the torches DID turn up in the end – in a box, hidden under hundreds of PACKETS OF CRISPS!!!

When I'm sure everyone is asleep,
I write a note to Beans using the
picture code.

I pop my head out of our cabin, check
the COAST IS CLEAR and slip the
note under his door.

I am sure that Laura will stop at *nothing* to **WIN** the **ACE ADVENTURERS' PRIZE!**

And as Fred Fantastic always says, **FOLLOW THAT HUNCH!**

 We have TWO clues: first the campfire story sabotage, now the hidden torches. But we can only solve this case when we have **PROOF**.

I'm doing a wordsearch in my puzzle book under the covers, but I can hardly concentrate.

Tomorrow is our last day. Our last chance to win some points.

Our last chance to solve the CASE OF THE ACE ADVENTURERS' PRIZE!

FRIDAY

Up early, and the sun is shining.

The final activity is announced...

THE EXTREME SPORTS CHALLENGE!!

There are **big** points to be won.

The whistle goes and with a mighty **cheer** the challenge begins.

The first challenge is

GLADIATORS
WITH
INFLATABLES.

We are each paired against someone from another team. We get up on to a bouncy-castle platform and have to knock our opponent off it using a

GIANT
inflatable fruit!

105

I am paired opposite Nadia.

She NEARLY knocks me off with a

HUGE

strawberry

and I **wobble** on the edge...

But then I JUST get in a good move with my **giant cucumber** and Nadia falls off. She is **laughing**. Nadia is a good sport.

The second challenge is wriggling through different plastic tunnels. Alisha is the smallest in our team and she is SO FAST, like a

speedy burrowing mole!

The final and **biggest** challenge is the timed circuit run. We all crowd around to study the map. Coloured chalk signs mark the route.

CIRCUIT RUN

high ropes

Pond

woods

quiet area

play area

Snowy Owl Cabin →

Dormouse Cabin →

Golden Eagle Cabin →

Gazelle Cabin →

log seating

FINISH

games barn

canteen

START

We each set off at regular intervals.
I am lining up, waiting to begin, and I find myself standing next to Laura.

I am just bending down to re-tie my shoelaces, when I catch a glimpse of her *hands* – covered in

coloured chalk.

STRANGE.

I am just opening my mouth to say something when the whistle goes and it's my turn to set off.

I start out at a **_good pace,_** and overtake quite a few other runners.

I reach the sign **pointing LEFT.**

I run past the pond, away from the dark woods with the others close behind.

This isn't the **right** route, **surely???**

I think *puff puff*

There is something funny going on...

puff puff

Then the penny drops!

Someone has turned the signs round – just like in that episode of **FRED FANTASTIC!!!!!!!**

AND I KNOW WHO IT WAS...

BUT – it makes **n🅞** sense! How does this help Laura win the race?

I start running *faster* and *faster* – I must find Beans!

My heart is **pounding** and my legs feel like

wobbly jelly,

but I keep going...

And AT LAST I reach the finishing line.

The **Ace Adventure Helpers** use their stopwatches to work out our times. Everybody is rushing over to the scoreboard, but I am rushing in the **OPPOSITE DIRECTION** to find Beans.

It takes AGES, but at last I finally find him in the crowd.

I tell Beans about how Laura changed the signs to alter the running race route. It takes a while as I still have hardly got my breath back!

"But WHY???" he asks.

"Her team had to follow the same signs as we did – it didn't help them win. So why did she do it? **What IS she up to?**"

This case is a **HOT POTATO!** FRED
FANTASTIC says this a lot. It doesn't
mean it's a real potato...

It means it's a **super-tricky** problem.

And slowly it begins to dawn on me...
Maybe we've got it wrong. Maybe it's
not about the **ACE ADVENTURERS'**
PRIZE at all.

"The answer is in the **clues** if only we

could just see it," I say. "Laura ruined my night-time campfire **spooky** story..."

"And she hid the torches to spoil the **moonlight** walk..." says Beans.

"And she made us run around the pond instead of through the **dark** woods," I say...

And suddenly I have a

LIGHT-BULB MOMENT!!!

"I've GOT it!

I KNOW what's happened!" I say.
"Laura is afraid of

THE DARK!"

And we put together the pieces of
the puzzle. So we were right all along
about what Laura did, but not about
WHY.

We rush over to Mr D and tell him all about it.

Mr D listens quietly, but he just says, "Just give me a few minutes." We see him walk with Laura over to the Quiet Area for a chat.

Now Mr D and Laura are coming back over to us.

Laura looks at her shoes and says, very quietly, "I'm sorry I ruined the activities for everyone. I didn't want you all to know that I think the dark is **really scary.**"

"But all those camps you've been to," I say, "night-kayaking in the Amazon, sleeping under the stars in the Arctic!"

Laura digs a little hole in the mud with her toe and says nothing. I now see that might have been a bit of an **exaggeration.**

I can't help feeling sorry for her.

So I say, "Well, not many people know this, but I used to be really **scared** of my dressing-gown, hanging on my bedroom door.

I thought it would

come to life

in the

night!"

I shudder. Beans pulls his T-shirt over his head and does a creepy *dressing-gown* dance around me. Laura smiles.

"Come on," says Beans, "they're announcing the **winners!**" and we all go over together.

Kirstie and Amy's team wins the **Ace Adventurers' Prize**, which they really deserve because they scored well on the activities, but also Amy was brave and Kirstie was kind.

We all **CLAP** and **CHEER.**

I see Laura clapping too.

I scored some extra points with my **super-fast running,** so our team is **second,** which is

PRETTY FANTASTIC!

Now it is time to pack our bags and get back on to the coach. With the Helpers waving us off, we head back home.

As we come round the corner and see our school, there are our families waiting for us.

McClusky is beside himself with **excitement** to see me!

Welcome home, Dot!

We are all very **GRUBBY** and **TIRED**

and are walking a bit like

ZOMBIES.

Joe could not find his shorts anywhere and is wearing his pyjama bottoms.

For a reason absolutely no one can explain, Frankie seems to be absent-mindedly wearing TWO pairs of shorts, one **on top** of the other.

Mr D makes sure Joe is reunited with his shorts, Lily and Amber are wearing the right shoes and Fiyaz has his tooth safely in his pocket...

And as the last of us are leaving...

I see Mr D walking to his car to go home, and he does a little

dance of joy,

probably because he **loved** the school trip SO MUCH.

So tired, can hardly write a single word.
My own home. My own bed.

Saturday

Today is the

LARKS
IN THE
PARK Dog Show.

And here is McClusky's surprise –
Mum has given him an AMAZING
new **bow tie!** Made out of the
spinning mini-windmill from his

hoard of treasures! (See, there IS a point keeping loads of stuff, I tell Mum.)

I brush McClusky's coat. He looks very cool with a **quiff** and he is SO PROUD of his new bow tie.

Me and Beans go over to the dog show while Mum and the twins look at the homemade jams.

When we arrive, there are lots of dogs already waiting...

"Come on, McClusky, it's **starting!**"

He parades beautifully in the

HANDSOMEST HOUND

round, and wags his tail until it is an absolute *blur*.

And now the trickiest round: the

Sausage-on-a-plate Race.

The contestants are lining up.

I give McClusky his plate and his sausage. I stare at him **very intensely** and he stares back.

"You can do it, McClusky!" I say.

Then the whistle is blown and they all set off.

But now lots of people crowd in front of me and I lose sight of McClusky.

I am hopping up and down, but I can't see over everybody's heads – it is **SO FRUSTATING** – until at last I hear the applause and cheers and the judge calls out:

"We HAVE A WINNER!"

Later, we are all sitting on the grass having ice creams. McClusky is wearing his BEST IN SHOW rosette.

"First place in the

Sausage-on-a-plate Race,

McClusky!" I say.

"He also scored points for being
a **handsome hound** AND for his
tail-wagging!" says Beans.

"His new bow tie must have given
him lots of last-minute confidence,"
I say.

We talk about **THE CASE OF THE ACE
ADVENTURERS' PRIZE.** This was our
trickiest yet!

"It turns out that Laura isn't nearly as confident as she makes out," I say, "and Amy is getting **braver** every day!"

"Yes!" says Beans. And then he says, "I wonder what Norman is doing right now..."

Another case...

What will our next fiendishly tricky mystery be?

Have you read?

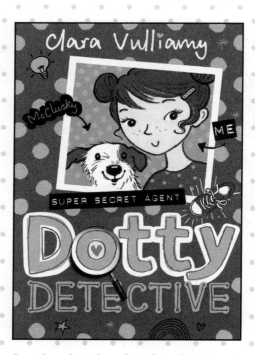

When someone seems set on sabotaging the school show, Dot is determined to find out how, and save the day!

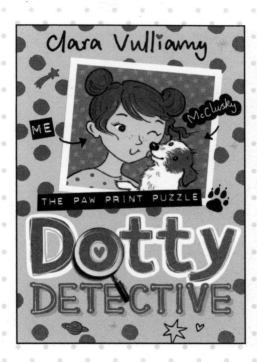

When Dot starts hearing strange noises at night, Beans is convinced there has to be something SPOOKY afoot. But before they can be certain Dot and Beans must GET PROOF.

Join Dot, Beans and McClusky
on their next case...

LOOK OUT FOR ANOTHER

Dotty DETECTIVE

coming soon...